First published 2014 by Walker Books Ltd, 87 Vauxhall Walk, London SE11 5HJ

This edition published 2015

2 4 6 8 10 9 7 5 3 1

© 2014 Jenni Desmond

The right of Jenni Desmond to be identified as author/illustrator of this work has been asserted
by her in accordance with the Copyright, Designs and Patents Act 1988

This book has been typeset in Melior

Printed in China

British Library Cataloguing in Publication Data:
a catalogue record for this book is available from the British Library

ISBN 978-1-4063-6074-5

www.walker.co.uk

FOR JO AND ADRIAN ♡

THE ZEBRA WHO RAN TOO FAST

JENNI DESMOND

WALKER BOOKS

AND SUBSIDIARIES

LONDON • BOSTON • SYDNEY • AUCKLAND

Zebra had two best friends, Elephant and Bird.
They were three best friends together.

Elephant knew lots of curious facts. Zebra and Bird could listen to him for hours.

Bird was so funny he made Zebra and Elephant laugh until they cried and hiccuped.

And Zebra knew the best games
and was the fastest runner of them all.
He was always cheerful and lively and bouncy.

But one gusty day, Zebra was so cheerful and lively
and bouncy that he ran TOO fast.
It made Elephant and Bird very dizzy.
Very dizzy indeed.
"Stop," said Bird.
"Stop," said Elephant.
But Zebra would not stop.

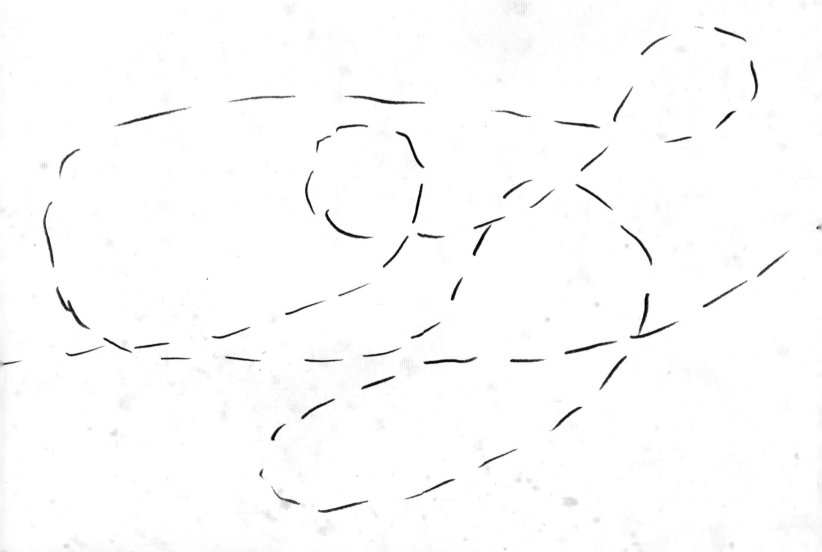

weeeee!

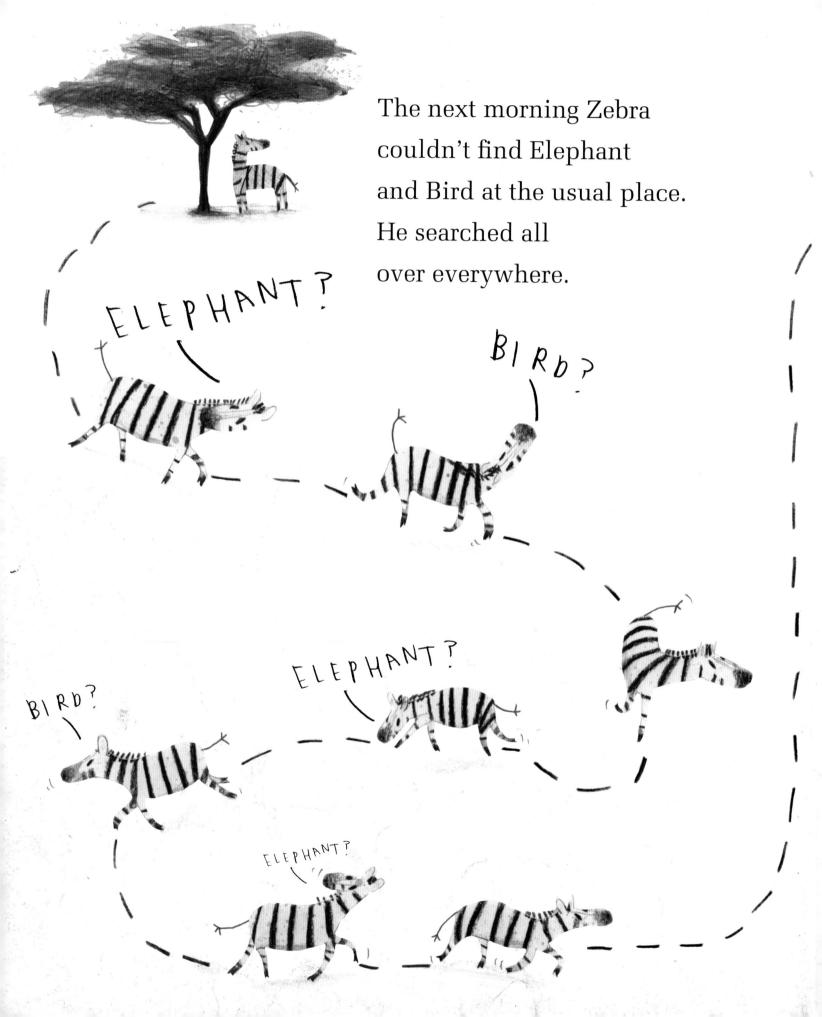

The next morning Zebra couldn't find Elephant and Bird at the usual place. He searched all over everywhere.

HELLOOOOO !

At last he found them in the pool.

"Shall we play my new circle-running game?" said Zebra.
But Elephant and Bird just walked off.
"We don't want to play with you," they said.
"You make us dizzy!"

Zebra didn't know what to do.

The day was long and hot. The air was heavy.
Zebra didn't feel like playing any more.
He stood and wondered what Elephant and Bird
were doing without him.

"I can't even reach the leaves on the tree by myself," he thought sadly.

"I'm hungry and I miss my friends.
I wish I'd listened to them."
Zebra thought he might be
on his own for the rest of his life.

Then Giraffe came along.

HELLO.

HELLO.

"Hello," said Giraffe.
"If you eat something you'll feel much better."

Giraffe was right. He was very kind
and wise. Zebra felt a little better.
"Do you want to play my new
circle-running game?" he said.

jump

jump

run run run run run

Zebra and Giraffe chased and
chased each other.
Giraffe could run even faster than Zebra.
Zebra almost didn't miss Elephant
and Bird any more.

jump

That night a fierce storm came. Zebra and Giraffe
were too busy running to notice.

But Elephant and Bird were frightened of storms.
Elephant's ears were hurting and Bird was in tatters.
"I wish we could play one of Zebra's games," said Bird.

"We have to find him," said Elephant, and they set off searching all over everywhere.

They found him with Giraffe.
"We have missed you," said Elephant.
"We're sorry for leaving you alone," said Bird. "We're scared."

"Don't be scared," said Zebra. "My new game
will make you feel much better. This time
I promise not to run too fast."

Afterwards Elephant told them lots of interesting things. And then Bird told a joke that was so funny they all laughed and cried and hiccuped until they were completely exhausted.

The next day they all woke up in the sunshine. "I'm so happy that we're three best friends again," said Elephant to Zebra.

Zebra looked at Elephant for a long time.
"I don't know if we *can* be three best
friends any more," he said.

"Because now we're four best friends!
Four best friends together."
And Bird flew in and out of Giraffe's legs
and made them all laugh.

Jenni Desmond

is an illustrator, artist and picture book author.

Her aim is to make her illustrations entertaining, beautiful and funny.

Jenni graduated with distinction from the Masters in Children's
Book Illustration at Cambridge School of Art (APU).

Her first picture book won the 2013 Cambridgeshire "Read It Again!"
Picture Book Award, and in 2014 she was the illustrator of the
Family Trail at the National Portrait Gallery BP Portrait Award.

Jenni lives in Hackney, London.